If I Were A TREE, What Would I Be?

Margaret Cheasebro

Illustrated by Ayin Visitacion

Balboa Press books may be ordered through booksellers or by contacting:

Balboa Press
A Division of Hay House
1663 Liberty Drive
Bloomington, IN 47403
www.balboapress.com
1 (877) 407-4847

Because of the dynamic nature of the Internet, any web addresses or links contained in this book may have changed since publication and may no longer be valid. The views expressed in this work are solely those of the author and do not necessarily reflect the views of the publisher, and the publisher hereby disclaims any responsibility for them.

ISBN: 978-1-9822-4009-7 (sc)
ISBN: 978-1-9822-4010-3 (e)

Library of Congress Control Number: 2019920758

Print information available on the last page.

Balboa Press rev. date: 12/18/2019

BALBOA.PRESS
A DIVISION OF HAY HOUSE

This page is dedicated to all the people who love trees and have shared with me how much trees mean to you. All of you inspire me.

"Hi, Francisco. Come walk with me while I visit one of my tree friends."

"You like trees? I had no idea, Katie. So do I!"

"I have talks with my tree friends," said Katie. "I hear them with my heart."

"That's where I hear them too!" Francisco sounded excited.

"I love this meadow. See that big cottonwood, Francisco? That's Grandfather Tree, one of my favorite trees."

"What a huge trunk! And there are so many big, leafy branches," said Francisco. "This tree must be very old."

"And very wise. We like each other." Katie smiled at the tree.

"I think it's cool to have tree friends," said Francisco.

"If I were a tree, I would be your friend," Katie told him.

"If I were a tree, I would be your friend too." Francisco thought for a moment. "But I already am your friend!"

Katie smiled. "The tree is happy that we're friends. My heart feels warm, like sunshine."

"My heart feels good too," Francisco said with a grin. "I'm glad the tree likes me!"

"Grandfather Tree, we'll play in the meadow under your branches," said Katie.

"We'll make pretty designs with rocks in your shade," Francisco told the tree.

"I'll make a chain of flowers to string around your trunk," Katie added.

"If I were a tree, I would say thank you by singing to you as the wind whistled through my leaves." Francisco cocked his head. "Listen! I hear the song!"

"Sometimes at night it feels like I'm snuggled in the tree's branches, being rocked to sleep." Katie closed her eyes and thought about how good that felt.

"I would sit up there on that big branch and tell funny stories so the tree wouldn't get lonely," said Francisco.

"If I were a tree, I'd listen to your stories and laugh at the funny parts," Katie replied.

"I wonder what a tree sounds like when it laughs," said Francisco. "Maybe its leaves rustle like a giggle."

"Sometimes I tell the tree what makes me sad," Katie said quietly.

"If I were a tree, I would know when you are sad and give you a hug with my branches," Francisco replied.

Katie nodded. "If the tree had a little sore, I would put a bandage on the sore. I would kiss the tree and say, 'Get well soon'."

"If I were a tree, I would be happy to see you coming," Francisco said. "Oh! Can you feel that in your heart? The tree likes having us as friends."

"I feel like I'm glowing inside," Katie said. "I love this feeling!"

"I will have to visit Grandfather Tree more often," said Francisco. "I like this feeling too."

"If I were a tree, I would shake my branches with excitement when you come to visit,"

Katie told him.

"If I were a tree, I would listen when you have something to tell me," Francisco said.

"And I would listen to the tree," Katie replied. "This cottonwood knows what to whisper to my heart."

"Once when I visited my favorite tree, I was upset," Francisco told her. "A boy said something mean to me at school. It hurt my feelings."

"I'm sorry someone treated you that way," Katie said.

"The tree told me to stand tall, because it knows what a really cool person I am," said Francisco. "The next time that boy said something mean, it didn't hurt so much because I remembered what the tree told me."

"We're lucky to have such good tree friends" Katie said.

"If I were a tree, Katie, I would teach you things to help you become wiser."

"Like what?" asked Katie.

"Like how to feel more grounded," Francisco said. "Then you will feel like your feet are stuck to the ground, almost like a magnet. That way, you can think about what's happening right now and not worry about what might happen tomorrow or what happened yesterday."

"How do you feel more grounded?" asked Katie.

"Imagine a golden light coming from above your head through the top of your skull," said Francisco. "Then think about it flowing through your body and out the bottoms of your feet into the ground."

"Let me try that!" Katie squeezed her eyes shut. "It works! I feel glued to the ground. If I try that in school, my teacher might quit telling me to stop daydreaming."

"Listen," said Francisco. "The tree is telling us to love the ground. That will make it easier to stay grounded."

"Trees are so wise!" Katie said.

"They know lots of ways to help us," Francisco replied.

"We can help them too," said Katie. "One day someone dug a big hole beside Grandfather Tree. I was afraid that might hurt the tree, so I got a shovel and filled the hole with dirt."

"We can bring the tree water when it hasn't rained for a while," Francisco suggested.

"If I were a tree, I would be grateful and tell you thanks," said Katie.

"I have to go home now," Francisco said, "but I'll come back and visit you soon, Grandfather Tree."

"Look! The branches are waving at us," Katie cried with delight.

"If I were a tree, I would trust that we really will come back and visit," Francisco said.

"Goodbye, Grandfather Tree. I love you," said Katie. "We really will come back."

"Look, Katie! Grandfather Tree is smiling at us."

About the Author

Margaret Cheasebro has been a writer since she was nine years old when she began penning stories about her cats and dogs. Since then, she has been a journalist, newspaper editor, freelance writer, and elementary school counselor. She has won many state and national awards for her writing. She has always loved to climb trees. Now that she is retired, she doesn't do much tree climbing anymore, but she enjoys being around trees very much. She has a master's degree in psychology, counseling and guidance from the University of Northern Colorado in Greeley and a Ph.D. in metaphysics from the American Institute of Holistic Theology in Birmingham, Alabama. Her two most recent books, a young adult fantasy novel called The Healing Tree and a non-fiction book titled Healing with Trees: Finding a Path To Wholeness, both emphasize how helpful and satisfying it is to spend time around trees.